The Story Girl

Book 3

S0-BNW-804

To the Peterson
family with ♥,

Barbara Pavel

From the author of Anne of Green Gables

L.M. Montgomery

The Story Girl™

Book 3

SUMMER SHENANIGANS

First Baptist Church Library
53953 CR 17
Bristol, IN 46507

Adapted by Barbara Davoll

Zonder**kidz**

Zonder**kidz**.

The children's group of Zondervan

www.zonderkidz.com

Summer Shenanigans
© 2004 The Zondervan Corporation, David Macdonald, trustee and
Ruth Macdonald

Requests for information should be addressed to:
Grand Rapids, Michigan 49530

Library of Congress Cataloging-in-Publication Data pending

ISBN 0-310-70600-9 (pbk. ; alk. paper)

"The Story Girl" and *"L. M. Montgomery"* are trademarks of Heirs of L. M.
Montgomery Inc., used under license by The Zondervan Corporation.

"Summer Shenanigans" is adapted from *"The Story Girl"* by L. M.
Montgomery. Adaptation authorized by David Macdonald, trustee, and
Ruth Macdonald, the heirs of L. M. Montgomery.

Photograph of L. M. Montgomery used by permission of L. M. Montgomery
Collection, Archival and Special Collections, University of Guelph Library.

All rights reserved. No part of this publication may be reproduced, stored
in a retrieval system, or transmitted in any form or by any means—elec-
tronic, mechanical, photocopy, recording, or any other—except for brief
quotations in printed reviews, without the prior permission of the publisher.

Zonderkidz is a trademark of Zondervan

Editor: Gwen Ellis
Interior design: Susan Ambs
Art direction: Laura Maitner

04 05 06 07 /❖OP/ 10 9 8 7 6 5 4 3 2 1

Contents

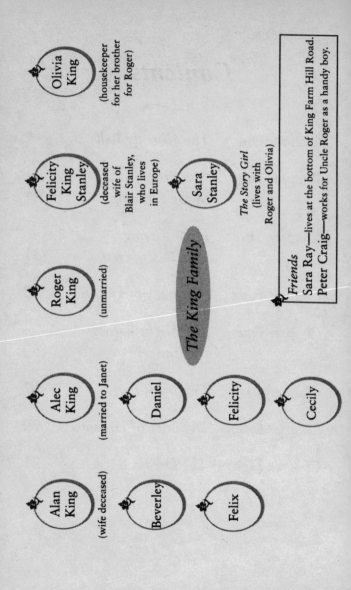

The King Family

Alan King (wife deceased)

Alec King (married to Janet)

Roger King (unmarried)

Felicity King Stanley (deceased wife of Blair Stanley, who lives in Europe)

Olivia King (housekeeper for her brother for Roger)

Beverley

Felix

Daniel

Felicity

Cecily

Sara Stanley
The Story Girl (lives with Roger and Olivia)

Friends
Sara Ray—lives at the bottom of King Farm Hill Road.
Peter Craig—works for Uncle Roger as a handy boy.

The Ghostly Bell

"There's—something—in the house,
ringing a bell," said Peter, in a shaky
voice. Even the Story Girl herself could
not have said that word something *with*
more creepy horror than Peter did.

Chapter One

t was a comfortable summer day in the King household. All of us cousins were enjoying the beauty of "being on our own" because the grown-ups, except for Uncle Roger, were away visiting Uncle Edward's family. Uncle Roger was in charge of us, but he was a Prince Edward Island farmer and busy in his fields. Peter, his handy boy, was helping Uncle Roger hoe potatoes. We always missed Peter when he had to work because he was so much fun. But Sara Stanley, one of our cousins (we called her the Story Girl), was at her very best on that Friday. She entertained us by telling one story after another.

The Story Girl sparkled her way through several tales that set our heads spinning. The one we liked best was about an Oriental princess who followed her bridegroom to war disguised as a boy—a page. What an adventure that was. The girls loved that one best, but we boys liked the one about a brave lady who danced with a robber on a moonlit road in Scotland. Sara really got into her stories. And each time she finished one, we would be sad and always beg for another.

Our cousin Cecily and her friend Sara Ray were off in a huddle, working on a "sweet" new knitted lace pattern they had found in an old magazine. We guys didn't see anything particularly *sweet* about it, but they did. What we thought was *sweet* were their secret whispers as they knitted. We learned "accidentally" that Sara Ray had named an apple for Johnny Price. This was a fad the girls had—each naming an apple for her *beau* or the boy she liked. If the apple had eight seeds in it, she would know that he loved her. Silly stuff! But you know how girls are. Cecily admitted in a secret whisper that Willie Fraser had written on his slate:

"If you love me as I love you,
No knife can cut our love in two."

"But, Sara Ray, *never* breathe this to a living soul," Cecily begged. "Willie even *showed* it to me." Cecily would have cut out her tongue if she had known we were listening behind the door. We could hardly contain ourselves and ran outside to laugh. "Just wait till we tell Peter," we howled.

Paddy, the Story Girl's cat, distinguished himself that day by catching a rat. He was terribly conceited about it—until Sara Ray cured his conceit by calling him a "dear, sweet cat." When she kissed him between the ears, he ran off. That was the last straw. He resented being called a *sweet* cat.

That cat had a sense of humor. Very few cats have. Most of them will slink around you, purring no matter what you say. But Paddy was a tasteful cat. The Story Girl would pretend to box his ears with her fist and say, "Bless your little gray heart, Paddy. You're a good old rascal," and Paddy would purr with satisfaction.

I used to take a handful of the skin on his back, shake him gently, and say, "Pat, you're a wise old cat. You've forgotten more than any human being ever knew." Paddy would lick his chops with delight. But to be called a *sweet* cat! Never!

It was the day before our grown-ups came home, and Felicity tried a new cake recipe that was very complicated. It was enough to make your mouth water. While we were finishing the last of our delicious cake at the tea table, Dan made an announcement. "Peter says the red raspberries are ripe. How about we go pick some after we finish our tea."

"I'd like to," sighed Felicity. "But we'd come home tired and then have all the milking to do. You boys had better go alone."

"Peter and I will do the milking for one evening," said Uncle Roger. "You can all go. Then Felicity can make a raspberry pie for supper tomorrow night to welcome your folk's home." That sounded good to all of us. It would be fun to pick the berries and a nice surprise for the aunts and uncles when they returned.

Right after supper, we all set off carrying buckets and jugs. Felicity brought along a small basket full of jelly cookies "just in case." We went to the maple tree grove on the back of Uncle Roger's farm. It was a pretty walk through a world of green, whispering tree branches and sweet-smelling ferns. Sunlight shone through the woods, making beautiful patterns on the ground as we walked. The raspberries were perfectly ripe, and in no time, we had our buckets and jugs full.

Stuffing ourselves with the delicious berries, we stopped by a spring in the woods where we ate the jelly cookies and refreshed ourselves with cool drinks of water. While we rested, the Story Girl told us a tale about a haunted spring up in the mountains where a lovely fairy lady lived.

"If you drank a cup of the water with her," said the Story Girl, her eyes glowing in the twilight, "you were never seen in the world again. You were whisked away to fairyland and lived there the rest of your life. You never wanted to come back because when you drank from the magic cup, you forgot all of your past life."

"I wish there was such a place as fairyland," said Cecily, "and a way to get to there."

"There *is* such a place, Cece," the Story Girl replied. "And I think there is a way of getting there too, if we could only find it."

Well, the Story Girl was right. There is such a place as fairyland—but only children can find the way to it. And they don't know that it is fairyland until they have grown so old that they forget the way. Only a few who remain children at heart can find it because it lies in the imagination. The world calls those who find it poets, artists, and storytellers. But we know they are just people like us who have never forgotten the way to fairyland.

As we sat there, the Awkward Man passed by with his gun over his shoulder and his dog at his side. He did not look like an awkward man there in the heart of the maple woods. He strode along masterfully and lifted his head like a king.

The Story Girl threw him a kiss, and the Awkward Man took off his hat and bowed to her gracefully.

"I don't understand why they call him an awkward man," said Cecily when he was out of earshot.

"You'd understand why if you ever saw him at a party or a picnic," said Felicity in her snooty way. "He falls all over himself whenever a woman looks at him. He can't even pass the plates of food without dropping them. They say it's pitiful to see him."

"I must get acquainted with that man next summer," said the Story Girl. "If I put it off any longer, it will be too late. I'm growing so fast that Aunt Olivia says I'll have to wear ankle skirts next summer. If I begin to look grown-up, he'll be frightened of me, and then I'll never learn about the Golden Milestone mystery."

"Do you think he'll ever tell you who Alice is?" I asked.

"I think I know who Alice is already," the Story Girl said. But she would tell us no more. She loved to work out a mystery and save it in her brain until she could tell us a wonderful story about it. Sometimes she was too much!

When the jelly cookies were all eaten, it was time to head for home. There are places more comfortable than a forest—even if it has an enchanted spring—when it gets dark. We walked quickly through the forest in the shadowy darkness and entered the King orchard. In the middle of it, between the rows of trees, we met Peter. There was just enough light for us to see that his face was white with terror.

"Peter, what's the matter?" cried Cecily.

"There's—*something*—in the house, ringing a *bell*," said Peter, in a shaky voice. Even the Story Girl herself could not have said that word *something* with more creepy horror than Peter did.

We all drew close together. I felt a shivery feeling along my back, which I had never known before. If Peter had not been so frightened, we might have thought he was trying to play a joke on us. But he was truly terrified.

"Nonsense!" said Felicity, but her voice shook. "There isn't a bell in the house to ring. You must have imagined it, Peter. Or else Uncle Roger is trying to fool us."

"Your uncle Roger went to Markdale right after milking," said Peter. "He locked up the house and gave me the key. I'm sure there wasn't a soul inside when I heard the ringing. I drove the cows up to the pasture and got back about fifteen minutes ago. Then, I sat down on the front steps for a minute, and all at once, I heard a bell ring eight times in the house. I tell you—I was skeered. I made a bolt for the orchard, and you won't catch me going near that house 'til your uncle Roger comes home."

You wouldn't have caught any of us going near it either. We were almost as badly scared as Peter. We were all huddled together in a pitiful little group. Oh, what an eerie place that orchard was then. What shadows! What noises! Spooky bats swooped down close by. We had seen them before and paid no attention. They were just part of the business of living in the country. But tonight there were more of them. We *couldn't* look in every direction at once, and goodness only knew what might be *behind* us!

"There *can't* be anybody in the house," said Felicity.

15

"Well—go see for yourself," replied Peter, handing her the key.

Felicity had no intention of going and seeing.

"Boys are supposed to be braver than girls."

"But we ain't," said my brother, Felix. "I'm not much scared of anything *real*, but a *haunted house* is a different thing."

"Who says it's haunted," scoffed the Story Girl. "There's some explanation for it. Nothing like this has ever happened in our family. The Kings have always been respectable people."

"Wh—what about our *family* ghost, Emily King?" whispered Felix.

"She never appeared anywhere but the orchard," replied the Story Girl practically.

"Oh look!" said Cecily in a fearful whisper, pointing toward Uncle Alec's tree. "What is that white thing floating?"

"That's my old apron," answered Felicity. "I hung it there today when I was gathering eggs. Oh, what will we do? Uncle Roger had lots of things to pick up in town. He may not be back for hours. I can't believe there's anything in the house."

"Maybe it's only old Peg Bowen," suggested Dan.

There wasn't much comfort in that thought. We were almost as afraid of Peg Bowen as we would have been of a ghost.

16

Peter scoffed at the idea. "Peg Bowen wasn't in the house before your uncle Roger locked it up. How would she have gotten in afterward?" he said. "No, it isn't Peg Bowen. It's something that *walks*."

Not thinking how it would scare the girls, I said, "Well, Peg Bowen walks. We've seen . . ."

I stopped short midsentence when I saw the girls' faces.

"I know a story about a ghost," said the Story Girl, trying to change the subject. "It's about . . ."

"Don't!" cried Cecily hysterically, clapping her hand over the Story Girl's mouth. "Don't you dare say another word! I can't bear it!"

The Story Girl didn't. But she had said enough. There were never in all the world six more badly scared kids than the King cousins who huddled in the old orchard that August night.

All at once *something* leapt from a branch of the tree above us and lighted on the ground. We split the air with our screams and tried to run, only to knock each other down as we frantically ran into each other. Then we saw with shame that it was only Paddy cat.

"Here, old Pat," I said, picking him up. I felt a certain comfort in his soft solid body. "Stay with us, old fellow," I said, stroking him. But even Paddy was acting weird. He squirmed away from me with a loud meow of protest and disappeared with soundless leaps into the long grasses.

The moon rose slowly, but this only made matters worse. The shadows now moved and danced as the night wind tossed the branches of the trees. The old house, with its dreadful secret, was white and clear against the dark background of the pine trees. We were terribly tired but didn't dare sit down, as the grass was wet with dew.

"The family ghost has only been seen in the daylight," said the Story Girl.

"There's no such thing as a ghost," I said firmly. Oh, how I wished I could believe it!

"Then what rung that bell?" asked Peter. "Bells don't ring by themselves. 'Specially when there ain't anybody in the house to ring it."

"Oh—when will Uncle Roger come home!" sobbed Felicity. "I know he'll laugh at us, but it's better to be laughed at than scared like this."

Uncle Roger did not come 'til nearly ten. Never was there a more welcome sound than the rumble of his buggy wheels in the lane. We ran to the orchard gate and swarmed across the yard just as he got out.

"What now, Felicity?" he asked mockingly. "Have you tempted anyone to eat any more bad berries?" He chuckled, staring at us in the moonlight.

"Oh, Uncle Roger, don't go in," begged Felicity. "There's something dreadful in there—something that rings a bell. Peter heard it. Don't go in."

"Why not?" Uncle Roger asked, fitting the key into the lock. "What story have you been telling now, Story Girl?"

"I told it," confessed Peter. "I clearly heard a bell ringing."

As Uncle Roger unlocked the door, a clear, sweet bell rang out ten chimes.

"That's the bell I heard," yelled Peter stubbornly, falling backward off the step.

We had to wait until Uncle Roger stopped laughing before we heard the explanation. We thought he would *never* stop.

"That's Grandfather King's clock striking," he said as soon as he was able to speak. "Sammy Prott came along after tea, and I gave him permission to clean the old clock. He had it going in no time. And now it has almost frightened you poor little monkeys to death."

Uncle Roger had laughed at us before, but now we heard him chuckling all the way as he went out to the barn.

"I wouldn't mind if he'd laugh once and get over it," said Felicity bitterly. "But he'll laugh at us for a year and tell the story to every soul that comes to the place. That bell has never rung in my lifetime. Who would think it would be the clock? Now he'll tell it far and wide."

"You can't blame him for that," said the Story Girl. "I'll tell it too. I don't care if the joke is on me. A story is a story, no matter whom it's about. But it's hateful to be laughed at—and grown-ups always do it. I never will when I'm grown-up."

"I'm dreadful tired," sighed Cecily.

"Grown-ups may tease a lot, but it's comforting to have them around," said Felix.

"I'm ready for the aunts and uncles to come back," Felicity said. "I thought it would be lots of fun being in charge of the house and cooking, but I'm plumb tuckered out. And I've got to clean the whole house tomorrow and fix supper to welcome them home. I can't wait to see them and let them be responsible again."

Poor Cecily, who was still shook up, said, "I sure hope they enjoyed their vacation." As she started up the steps to bed, she called back over her shoulder, "I think *we* need a vacation too." We all agreed.

The Proof of the Pudding

First Baptist Church Library
53953 CR 17
Bristol, IN 46507

The slices were smooth and golden and looked appetizing smothered in Cecily's maple syrup. But even though none of us said anything, it just didn't taste quite right. It was tough—very tough—and lacked the richness of Aunt Janet's cornmeal pudding.

Chapter Two

The next morning Felicity was disgusting as she bustled around putting the house in order. You might have thought she was forty rather than fourteen. She *did* have a lot to do—but she didn't have to act like somebody had died and made her queen. She cleaned the whole house and threatened to do awful things if any one *moved* and stirred up any dust. Then she set about making an elaborate welcome-home supper. She trusted the other girls to make the meals for us during the day while she worked on the special dinner. We all agreed that the Story Girl should make a cornmeal pudding for lunch.

Sara Stanley had been taking cooking lessons from Felicity all week. She was doing fairly well, though she had made a good many mistakes, especially with bread making. But this morning, Felicity had no time to oversee her.

"You'll have to do the pudding yourself," Felicity said. "The recipe's so plain and simple you can't do it wrong. If there's anything you don't understand, you can ask me. But don't bother me if you can help it."

The Story Girl didn't bother her once. She made the pudding and delivered it to the lunch table all by herself. She was very proud of it and it looked beautiful. The slices were smooth and golden and looked appetizing smothered in Cecily's maple syrup. But even though none of us said anything, it just didn't taste quite right. It was tough—very tough—and lacked the richness of Aunt Janet's cornmeal pudding.

If it hadn't been for the sauce, it would have been very dry eating, but it was eaten right down to the last crumb. The rest of the meal wasn't perfect, but it was good. We all had enough to be pleasantly full, even without dessert.

"I wish I was twins so's I could eat more," said Dan, when he simply had to stop.

"What good would being twins do you?" asked Peter. "People who squint can't eat any more than people who don't squint, can they?"

"What has squinting got to do with twins?" asked Dan. None of us could see any connection between Peter's two questions.

"Why, twins are just people who squint, aren't they?" questioned Peter.

We thought he was trying to be funny and laughed at him until Peter got sulky. "I don't care," he said.

24

"How's a fellow to know? Tommy and Adam Cowan, over at Markdale, are twins; and they're both cross-eyed. So I s'posed that was what being twins meant. It's all very fine for you fellows to laugh. I never went to school half as much as you did, and you was brought up in Toronto too. If you'd worked like I have ever since you was seven and just went to school in the winter, there'd be lots of things you wouldn't know either."

"Never mind, Peter," said Cecily. "You know lots of things they don't."

But Peter was not to be comforted and went off in a snit. He couldn't endure being laughed at in front of Felicity. He didn't mind when all the rest cackled at him; but Felicity was different. When she laughed at him, he got really upset.

Felicity had finished the cleaning and had the dinner all ready, so she now decided to stuff two new pincushions she had been making for her room. We heard her ramming around out in the pantry. Soon she came out frowning.

"Cecily, do you know where Mother put the sawdust she emptied out of that old pincushion of Grandmother King's? I thought it was in the tin box in the pantry."

"It is," answered Cecily.

"But it isn't. There isn't a speck of sawdust in that box."

The Story Girl had a terrible expression of horror and shame on her face. She didn't need to confess. Had she just held her tongue, no one would have ever made the connection between the cornmeal pudding and the mysterious disappearance of the sawdust. She told me later that she would have kept quiet but for a horrible fear that sawdust might not be good for people to eat—especially if there were needles in it.

"Oh, Felicity," she said, her voice expressing her awful fear. "I . . . I . . . thought that stuff in the box was cornmeal—and I used it to make the pudding."

Felicity and Cecily starred blankly at the Story Girl. We boys began to laugh but were stopped by Uncle Roger. He was rocking himself back and forth with his hand pressed against his stomach.

"Oh," he groaned. "I've been wondering about these sharp pains I've been feeling ever since lunch. Now I know. I must have swallowed a needle—several needles, perhaps. I'm done for!"

The poor Story Girl turned pale. "Oh, Uncle Roger, could it really be? You couldn't have swallowed a needle without knowing it, could you? Surely it would have stuck in your tongue or teeth."

"I didn't chew the pudding," groaned Uncle Roger. "It was too tough—I just swallowed the chunks whole."

26

He groaned and twisted and doubled himself up. But he overdid it. He was not as good an actor as the Story Girl. Felicity looked scornfully at him.

"Uncle Roger, you are not one bit sick," she said deliberately. "You are just putting on."

"Felicity, if I die from the effects of eating sawdust pudding flavored with needles, you'll be sorry you said such a thing to your poor old uncle," he said. "Even if there were no needles in it, sixty-year-old sawdust can't be good for my tummy. I doubt if it was even clean."

"Well, you know the old saying: 'Everyone has to eat a peck of dirt in his lifetime,'" giggled Felicity.

"But nobody has to eat it all at once," retorted Uncle Roger with another groan. "Oh, Sara Stanley, I'm a thankful man that your aunt Olivia will be home tonight. One more day and you would surely have kilt us all. I believe you did it on purpose to have another story to tell."

Uncle Roger hobbled off to the barn, still holding his stomach.

"Do you think he really feels sick?" asked the Story Girl anxiously.

"No, I don't," answered Felicity. "You needn't worry over him. I'm sure there's nothing wrong at all. Mother sifted that sawdust very carefully, and I greatly doubt there would have been any needles left in it."

"I know a story about a man whose son swallowed a mouse," said the Story Girl.

"For cryin' out loud, Story Girl. You have a story for every occasion," remarked Felix.

Sara Stanley glowered at him and went on with her story.

"Anyway, this man had a problem. He went to the doctor's house and woke him up just as the tired doctor had fallen asleep."

"'Oh, Doctor, my son has swallowed a mouse,' he cried. 'What shall I do?'

"'Tell him to swallow a cat,' roared the poor doctor and slammed his door.

"Now if Uncle Roger has swallowed any needles, maybe it would make it all right if he swallowed a pincushion."

We all laughed, but Felicity soon grew sober.

"It seems awful to think of eating a sawdust pudding. How on earth did you make such a mistake?"

"It looked just like cornmeal," said the Story Girl, with her face turning red. "I'm going to give up trying to cook and stick to things I can do. And if any one of you ever mentions sawdust pudding to me, I'll never tell you another story as long as I live."

The threat worked. Never did we mention that unholy pudding. But the Story Girl couldn't keep the lid on Uncle Roger or the grown-ups. He tormented her for the rest of the summer. We never sat down at breakfast that he didn't ask if there was any sawdust in the cereal. Every time his rheumatism flared up, he claimed it was a needle traveling about in his body. And Aunt Olivia was warned to label all the pincushions in the house "Contents, sawdust; not intended for puddings."

How Kissing Was Discovered

*Bending down to her, his lips touched hers—
and then, he forgot all about the beautiful pebble and so did Aglaia. Kissing was discovered!*

Chapter Three

T he August evening was calm and golden. It was especially lovely for the grown-ups who were traveling home. Uncle Roger had gone to the station to meet them at sunset, and all of us were sitting on the cool grasses in the orchard near the Pulpit Stone. The dining-room table was waiting and ready—spread with food fit for a king. Felicity had really outdone herself. Only Peter was missing. We figured he was still sulking because we had teased him about "squinty" twins.

"It's been an interesting week, but I'm glad the grown-ups are coming back tonight. I've really missed Uncle Alec," remarked Felix.

"I wonder if they'll bring us anything," said Dan.

"I can't wait to hear about the wedding," said Felicity, who was braiding a flower necklace for Paddy.

"You girls are always thinking about weddings and getting married," said Dan with a scoff.

"Not so," said Felicity indignantly. "I am *never* going to get married. I think it is just horrid—so there!"

"I bet you'd think it more horrid to be an old maid," retorted Dan. He and Felicity were at it again, quarreling like brothers and sisters do.

"It depends on who you're married to," said Cecily seriously. "If you married a man like Father, it would be all right. But s'posen you married one like Andrew Ward? He's so mean and cross to his wife that she tells him every day that she wishes she'd never set eyes on him."

"Perhaps that's why he's mean and cross," said Felix.

"It isn't always the man's fault," said Dan in a dark tone. "When I get married, I'll be good to my wife, but I mean to be boss. When I open my mouth, my word will be law."

"If your word is as big as your mouth, I guess it will be," said Felicity cruelly.

"I pity the man who marries you, Felicity King," retorted Dan.

"Now, don't fight," begged Cecily.

"Who's fighting?" demanded Dan. "Felicity thinks she can say anything she likes to me, but I'll show her different." All of us knew he would do just that because we remembered when he ate the poisonous berries just to spite her. Another bitter spat would have occurred had the Story Girl not shown up just then.

"Felicity, what have you been doing to Peter?" she demanded. "He's up in the barn loft sulking and won't come down. He says it's your fault. You must have hurt his feelings."

"I don't know about his feelings," said Felicity, with an angry toss of her shining head. "But I guess I made his ears tingle all right; I boxed them both good and hard!"

"Oh, Felicity! What for?"

"Well, he tried to kiss me, that's what for!" said Felicity, turning very red. "As if I would let a hired boy kiss me! I guess Master Peter won't try anything like *that* again."

"Well, in that case," Sara Stanley said, "I think you did right to box his ears. Not because he's a hired boy but because it wouldn't be right for *any* boy to try it. That is unless you *invited* it," she said slyly, looking at her with amusement.

"You know better than that, Sara Stanley!" Felicity stormed. "No wonder you're called the Story Girl!"

"Cool yourself, Miss Felicity. You do a lot of queening around here—but you won't pull it off with me," retorted the Story Girl. "Now let's all settle down, and I'll tell you a story I read one time about how kissing was discovered." She had all of our attention immediately, including Felicity's.

"Didn't folks always know about kissing?" asked Dan.

"Not according to *this* story. It was discovered accidentally."

"Well, let's hear it then. I think kissing is awful silly now but maybe I won't when I'm a grown-up," he replied.

The Story Girl sat down with us on the grass and spread her skirt around her. Gazing dreamily up at the tinted sky, she began.

"It happened long, long ago in Greece, where so many other beautiful things happened. Before that, nobody had ever heard of kissing. And then it was just discovered in the twinkling of an eye. A man wrote it down, and the account has been preserved ever since.

"There was a young shepherd named Glaucon, a very handsome young shepherd, who lived in a little village called Thebes. It became a famous city afterward, but at that time it was only a little village—very quiet and simple. *Too* quiet for Glaucon's liking. He grew tired of it and thought he would liketo leave home and see the world. So he took his knapsack and his shepherd's crook and wandered away until he came to Thessaly.

"When he arrived in Thessaly, Glaucon got a job as a shepherd for a wealthy man. Every day

Glaucon had to lead the sheep up to pasture on Mount Pelion and watch them while they ate. While they were grazing, Glaucon passed the time by playing his flute. He played beautifully as he sat under the trees and watched the blue sea far off in the distance. As he played he thought about Aglaia, his master's daughter.

"She was so sweet and beautiful that Glaucon had fallen in love with her the first moment he saw her. When he was not playing his flute, he was dreaming that someday he might have sheep of his own and a dear little cottage down in the valley with Aglaia as his wife.

"Aglaia had fallen in love with Glaucon just as he had with her. But she never let on to him. He didn't know that often she would steal up the mountain and hide behind the rocks in the pasture. She loved to be near him and hear him play the beautiful music that came from his soul.

"One day Aglaia stepped on a branch noisily, and Glaucon discovered her crouching behind a rock, listening. It was amazing to him to find that she loved him. Since he was an honorable man, he told her father that they were in love; and Aglaia's father agreed that someday they could marry. After that, Aglaia came to the pasture every day. He would play for her, and together they would drive the sheep home.

"One day, Aglaia went up the mountain by a new way and came to a little brook. Something was sparkling brightly among its pebbles. Aglaia picked it up and found it was the most beautiful stone she had ever seen. It was only as large as a pea, but it glittered and flashed in the sunlight with every color of the rainbow. Aglaia was so delighted with it that she planned to give it as a present to Glaucon.

"Suddenly she heard a stamping of hooves behind her, and when she turned, she almost died from fright. For there was a goat named Pan, and he was terrible to see, looking more like a goat than a man. The goats like Pan were not beautiful, and nobody ever wanted to meet them face-to-face.

"'Give that stone to me,' said Pan, holding out his hand.

"But Aglaia, though she was frightened, would not give him the stone. 'I want it for Glaucon,' she said.

"'I must have it,' said Pan.

"He advanced threateningly, but Aglaia ran as hard as she could up the mountain. If she could only reach Glaucon, he would protect her. Pan followed her, clattering and bellowing, but in a few minutes, she rushed into Glaucon's arms.

"The dreadful sight of Pan and the awful noise he made frightened the sheep so badly that they ran off in all directions. When Glaucon begged Pan to stop frightening Aglaia and go away, Pan was furious, but grumbling loudly, he disappeared.

" 'Now dearest, what is all this trouble about?' Glaucon asked, still holding Aglaia tightly.

"When Aglaia was running from Pan, she had hidden the stone in her mouth, in case he should catch her. Now she removed it and told Glaucon the story. 'And I wanted to give it to you as a present,' she said.

"Glaucon reached for the stone that was glittering in the sunlight. But Aglaia, playing a game with him, popped the stone back into her mouth and poked it out between her red lips.

" 'Take it,' she said in fun. Glaucon did not want to let go of his sweetheart to take the stone. How was he to get it? Then he had a brilliant idea. He would take the beautiful stone from Aglaia's lips with his own lips.

"Bending down to her, his lips touched hers—and *then*, he forgot all about the beautiful pebble and so did Aglaia. Kissing was discovered!"

"That's quite a tale," said Dan. "I don't believe a word of it."

"Of course, we know it isn't really true," said Felicity.

"Well, I don't know," said the Story Girl thoughtfully. "I think there are two kinds of true things—

things that really *are* true and things that are not *really true*, but *might be*."

"I believe there's only one kind of trueness," said Felicity. "And anyway, this story couldn't be true. You know there is no such a thing as a goat like Pan."

"I wonder what became of the beautiful stone?" said Cecily.

"Likely Aglaia swallowed it," said my practical brother, Felix.

"Did Glaucon and Aglaia ever get married?" asked Sara Ray.

"The story doesn't say. It stops there," replied the Story Girl. "But of course they did. I will tell you what *I* think. I don't think Aglaia swallowed the stone. I think it just fell to the ground. After a while they found it, and it turned out to be of such value that Glaucon could buy all the flocks and herds in the valley and the sweetest cottage. He and Aglaia were married right away."

"But you only *think* that," said Sara Ray. "I'd like to be really sure what happened."

"Oh, fudge! None of it happened," said Dan. "I believed it while the Story Girl was telling the story. But I don't now.

"Listen! Are those wheels I hear in the driveway?"

Yes! Two wagons were driving up the lane. We rushed up to the house—and saw Uncle Alec, Aunt

Janet, and Aunt Olivia! The excitement was tremendous. Everybody was talking at once and hugging everyone else. Not until we were all seated around the supper table did we get to hear about the grownups' adventures in Nova Scotia.

"Well, I'm thankful to be home again," said Aunt Janet, beaming on us. "We had a real nice time and the wedding was beautiful. It was so nice for all of us brothers and sisters to be together—except for you, Roger," she added. "We all missed you. How did the children behave?"

We held our breath, waiting for his answer, thinking of all the bad things he could tell on us. "They were just little models," replied our kind uncle. "They were just as good as gold most of the time."

There were times when one couldn't help liking Uncle Roger.

Prophecy of Doom

A black list of sins—an endless list—rushed
through all of our young memories. For us
the Book of Judgment was already open,
and there we stood with no defense.

Chapter Four

he next day before noon, we were all in the orchard except Felix, who had gone to the post office.

Peter was complaining that he had to start taking the stumps out of the back field so they could plant elderberries. "Mr. Roger might have waited for cooler weather to do this. If it's this hot before noon, it will be broiling after lunch. And that's a fact!"

"Why don't you tell him so?" asked Dan.

"Ain't my business to tell him things," retorted Peter. "He says he always does it in August."

Sara Ray was staying the day with us because her mother had gone to town. She and the girls were eating timothy roots. I couldn't see how any plant's roots could taste good; but it was the newest fad, so the roots had to be eaten. The silly girls of Carlisle must have devoured tons of the tough, tasteless roots that summer.

Paddy was there also, padding about from one to the other of us on his black paws. The girls would stroke him and hold out a little bit of the timothy root to him. But ole' Pat would not even nibble. He had more sense than the girls. We all made over him a lot, stroking and petting him. All but Felicity, that is. She paid no attention to him at all because he belonged to the Story Girl, and they presently were not speaking to each other.

We boys were sprawling on the grass. Our morning chores had been done, and we had the whole day before us. We should have been feeling very comfortable and happy, but we weren't.

It had not been a pleasant week since Felicity and the Story Girl began spatting. On Monday a quarrel had risen between the two of them—none of us knew the cause. It remained a "dead secret" between them, and both seemed more bitter than usual. Nothing we did helped. None of our arguments or pleading, nor the tears of Cecily mixed with her prayers, seemed to have any effect.

"I don't know where you expect to go when you die, Felicity," Cecily said tearfully, "if you don't forgive people."

"I have forgiven her," was Felicity's answer, "but I am not going to speak to her first."

"It's very wrong, and more than that, it's so uncomfortable," complained Cecily. "It spoils everything."

"Were they ever like this before?" I asked Cecily, as we talked the matter over privately at Uncle Stephen's Walk in the orchard.

"Never for so long," said Cecily sadly. "They had a spell like this last summer, and one the summer before, but those only lasted a few days."

"And who spoke first?"

"Oh, the Story Girl. She got excited about something and spoke to Felicity before she thought, and then it was all right. But I'm afraid it isn't going to be like that this time. Haven't you noticed how careful the Story Girl is not to get excited? That is such a bad sign."

"We've just got to think of something," I said. "Felix and I will have to go home at the end of the summer, and it all will be spoiled if they are acting so silly and not talking."

"I'm—I'm praying about that," said Cecily in a low voice. Her tear-wet lashes lay trembling against her pale, round cheeks. Do you suppose it will do any good, Bev?"

"I think it probably will. Remember Sara Ray and getting money? That came from praying."

"I'm so glad you think so," Cecily replied in a teary voice. "Dan said it was no use for me to bother praying about it. He said if they *couldn't* speak, God might do something—but if they *wouldn't* speak, he

47

probably wouldn't interfere. Dan says such weird things. I'm afraid he's going to grow up just like Uncle Robert Ward, who never goes to church and doesn't believe more than half the Bible is true."

"Which half does he believe is true?" I inquired with curiosity.

"Oh, just the nice parts. He says there's a heaven all right, but no ... no ... hell. I don't want Dan to grow up like that. It isn't right. God can't let bad people into heaven, can he?"

"Well, no, I suppose not," I agreed, thinking of Billy Robinson, who cheated all of us with the Magic Seed scam.

"Of course, I can't help feeling sorry for those who have to go to *the other place*. But I suppose they wouldn't be comfortable in heaven either. They wouldn't feel at home. Andrew Marr said an awful thing one night last fall. Felicity and I were down there, and they were burning cornstalks. We were all standing around the bonfire, and he said he believed the other place must be lots more interesting than heaven because fires were jolly things. Now, did you ever hear the like?"

"I guess it depends a good deal on whether you're inside or outside the fires," I said.

"Oh, Andrew didn't mean it, of course. He just said it to sound smart and make us stare. The Marrs are all like that. But anyhow, I'm going to keep on praying that something will happen to make the Story Girl and Felicity forget their quarrel. I don't believe there is any use in praying that Felicity will speak first, because I'm sure she won't."

"But don't you suppose God could make her?" I said, feeling that it wasn't quite fair that the Story Girl should always have to give in and speak first. If she had spoken first the other times, it was surely Felicity's turn this time.

"I believe he could, but it would be more difficult. Anyway, I'm going to keep praying."

Peter, as was to be expected, took Felicity's part and said that the Story Girl ought to speak first since she was the oldest. That had always been his aunt Jane's rule.

Sara Ray thought Felicity should speak first because the Story Girl was half an orphan.

Felix tried to make peace between them and was put down like the rest of us. The Story Girl in a lofty way told him he was too young to understand. Felicity cruelly said that *fat* boys should mind their own business. After that, Felix declared it would serve Felicity right if the Story Girl never spoke to her again.

Dan had no patience with either of the girls, especially Felicity. "They both need a good spanking," he said. "But of course, that's only *my* opinion."

But a spanking wasn't likely to happen. None of the grown-ups even noticed their behavior, as the girls were not openly nasty to each other when the aunts and uncles were around. They had no idea what a pain their fighting was to us cousins or how it was spoiling our summer days, which were becoming fewer and fewer. Soon fall would come, and we would be on our way home to Toronto. How we wished we could all be as happy as we had been before the girls' silly feud.

The Story Girl had been making a flower wreath for her hair as we all sat around in the orchard. She now placed it on her head and looked up at Dan. "Maybe your opinion should be kept to yourself, Cousin. I knew a man once who always had his own opinion and . . ." The Story Girl got no further. We never heard the story of the man who always had his own opinion.

Felix came tearing up the lane with a newspaper in his hand. When a boy as fat as Felix runs at full speed on a broiling August day, he has a good reason.

"He must have gotten some bad news at the post office," remarked Sara Ray.

"Oh, I hope nothing has happened to Father," I exclaimed, springing anxiously to my feet. I had a sick, horrible feeling of fear running over me like a cold, rippling wave.

"It's just as likely to be good news," said the Story Girl, who was always optimistic and liked to think the best.

"He wouldn't be running so fast for good news," said Dan.

We were not in doubt long. The orchard gate flew open, and Felix crashed through. As soon as we saw his face, we knew he wasn't bringing good news. He had been running hard, and for a boy his size, he should have been red-faced. Instead he was white as a sheet. I was in such fear that I couldn't even find my voice to ask him what was the matter. It was Felicity who impatiently demanded an explanation:

"Felix King, what has scared you?"

Felix held out the newspaper—it was the Charlottetown *Daily Enterprise*.

"It's there," he gasped. "Look ... read ... Oh, do you ... think ... it's true? The ... end ... of ... the world ... is coming tomorrow ... at two o'clock ... in the afternoon!"

Crash! Felicity had been drinking from the precious blue and white cup that had hung on the well in the orchard for generations. It had been there forever, it seemed. Now it lay shattered on the ground, but no one paid any attention. At any other time, we would have been horrified to have the blue well cup broken, but now it didn't matter to any of us. What did it matter if all the antique well cups in the world were broken today if the world was coming to an end?

"Oh Sara Stanley, do you believe it? *Do you?*" gasped Felicity, clutching the Story Girl's hand. Cecily's prayer had been answered. In all the excitement, Felicity had spoken first. But this, like the breaking of the cup, had no significance for us at the moment.

The Story Girl snatched the paper and read the announcement to all of us who stood white, shaken, and silent—listening.

The headline read: "The Last Trump Will Sound at Two O'clock Tomorrow." The article had been written by a group in the United States that predicted August 12 would be Judgment Day. The article said the group's leader was encouraging group members to prepare for the end of the world by praying, fasting, and making white robes. It's funny to remember it now, but I will never forget the horror we felt in that sunny orchard that August morning. Keep in mind that we were only children and had a firm and simple faith that grown-ups knew far more than we did. We also believed that anything printed in a newspaper must be true.

"It can't be so," said Sara Ray, starting to cry as usual. "Do you believe it, Sara Stanley?"

"It *can't* be," said Felicity. "Everything looks just the same. Things can't look the same if Judgment Day is tomorrow."

"But that's just the way it is to come," I said, uncomfortable. "It says in the Bible that Judgment Day is to come like a thief in the night."

"But it also says in the Bible that nobody knows when the Judgment Day is to come—not even the angels in heaven," said Cecily eagerly. "Do you suppose the editor of the *Enterprise* knows something the angels in heaven don't even know? He's just a Grit [a Democrat], you know."

"I guess he knows as much about it as a Tory would," retorted the Story Girl. Uncle Roger's political persuasion was liberal, and Uncle Alec was a conservative. We cousins always argued for the political party of the older people who were the heads of our households.

"But it isn't really the *Enterprise* newspaper editor who is saying it," continued the Story Girl. "It's a man in the United States who claims to be a prophet. If he truly *is* a prophet, maybe he knows more than we do here in Canada."

"And it's in the newspaper too, in print just like the Bible," said Dan.

"Well, I'm going to depend on the Bible," said Cecily. "I don't believe it's the Judgment Day tomorrow—but I'm scared anyway."

That was exactly how we all felt. Just like the bell-ringing ghost, we didn't think it could be, but we were still afraid.

"I don't know," said Dan doubtfully. "The Bible was printed thousands of years ago, and that paper was printed this morning. It's more up-to-date."

"Yeah, but the Bible has been around for so long, it has to be true," remarked Felix.

"I want to do so many things," said the Story Girl. "But if it's the Judgment Day tomorrow, I won't have time to do any of them."

"It can't be much worse than dying, I s'pose," said Felix. He was grasping at anything that might bring him comfort.

"I'm awful glad I've got into the habit of going to church and Sunday school this summer," said Peter soberly. "I wish I'd made up my mind before this whether to be a Presbyterian or a Methodist. Do you s'pose it's too late now?"

"Oh, that doesn't matter," said Cecily earnestly. "If—if you're a Christian, Peter, that is all that's necessary."

"But it's too late for that," said Peter miserably. "I can't turn into a Christian between now and two o'clock tomorrow. I'll just have to be satisfied with making up my mind to be a Presbyterian or a Methodist. I wanted to wait 'til I got old enough to make out what was the difference, but I'll have to chance it now. I guess I'll be a Presbyterian, 'cause I want to be like the rest of you. Yes, I'll be a Presbyterian."

"I know a story about Judy Pineau and the word 'Presbyterian,'" said the Story Girl, "but I can't tell it now. If tomorrow isn't the Judgment Day, I'll tell it Monday."

"If I had known that tomorrow might be the Judgment Day, I wouldn't have quarreled with you last Monday, Sara Stanley, or been so horrid and sulky all week. Indeed, I wouldn't have," said Felicity, with unusual humility.

Felicity not only had spoken first, but here was a bit of an apology. So many amazing things were running through our heads, the things we would have done differently, "if we had only known." A black list of sins—an endless list—rushed through all of our young memories. For us the Book of Judgment was already open, and there we stood with no defense.

I thought of all the bad things I had done in my lifetime. I thought of when I had pinched Felix to make him cry out at family prayers, when I had played hooky from Sunday school and went fishing instead, and of a big fib—no, let's call it like it was—a big *lie*—I had told. I feared that the next day I might have to answer for all of them. Oh, how I wished I'd been a better boy!

Everyone else was thinking seriously too. "The quarrel was as much my fault as yours, Felicity," said the Story Girl, putting her arm around her friend. "We can't undo it now. But if tomorrow isn't the Judgment Day, we must be careful never to quarrel again."

"Oh, I wish my father were here," she continued. "I wonder if it is the Judgment Day in Europe where he is? Do you suppose I'll ever see him again?" she worried.

"You will," assured Cecily, who seemed to be our religious authority. "If it is the Judgment Day for Prince Edward Island, it will be for Europe and the whole world."

"I just wish we *knew*," said Felix desperately. "I'd do a whole lot better if I just knew."

Whom could we ask? Uncle Alec, our most trusted confidant, was away and would not be back until late that night. We didn't want to ask Aunt Janet nor Uncle Roger—worried that they would laugh and scoff at us. We were afraid of the Judgment Day, but we were also afraid of being laughed at.

"How about Aunt Olivia?" I asked.

"No, Aunt Olivia has gone to bed with a sick headache and mustn't be disturbed," said the Story

Girl. "Besides, what good would it do to ask the grown-ups? They don't know anything more about this than we do."

"But if they'd just say they didn't believe it, it would be sort of a comfort," said Cecily.

"I suppose the minister would know, but he's away on vacation," said Felicity. "Anyhow, I'll go and ask Mother what she thinks of it."

Felicity picked up the newspaper and headed for the house. We waited in agony for her return.

"Well, what did she say?" demanded Cecily when Felicity returned.

"She said, 'Run away and don't bother me. I don't have time for any of your nonsense,'" Felicity said in an injured tone. "When I said, 'The paper says tomorrow,' Ma just said, 'Judgment; Fiddlesticks!'"

"We'll just have to ask Uncle Roger," said Felix finally. This was definitely our last resort and our willingness to risk his ridicule showed how really desperate we were.

Uncle Roger was in the barnyard hitching his black mare to his buggy. His copy of the *Enterprise* newspaper was sticking out of his back pocket. We saw with sinking hearts that he seemed unusually sad. There was not a glimmer of a smile on his face.

"You ask him," said Felicity, nudging the Story Girl.

"Uncle Roger," said the Story Girl, her golden voice filled with fear and dread. "The newspaper says tomorrow is the Judgment Day. Do *you* think it is?"

"I'm afraid so," said Uncle Roger gravely. "The *Enterprise* is always very careful to print only reliable news."

"But Mother doesn't believe it," cried Felicity.

"That is just the trouble," he said shaking his head. "People won't believe it 'til it's too late. I'm going straight to Markdale to pay a man some money I owe him. After dinner, I'm going to Summerside to buy myself a new suit. My old one is too shabby for the Judgment Day."

He got into his buggy and drove away, leaving eight terrified souls behind him.

The Night Before the End

When we went to bed, it was a dark
stormy night. The rain was crying on the
roof as if the whole world was weeping
because its end was so near.

Chapter Five

Well, I suppose that settles it," said Peter in despair. "Tomorrow is Judgment Sunday."

"Is there anything we can do to *prepare*?" asked Cecily.

"I wish I had a white dress like you girls," sobbed Sara Ray. "Now it's too late to get one. Oh, I wish I had minded my Ma better. I wouldn't have disobeyed her so often if I'd thought Judgment Day was so near. When I go home, I'm going to tell her about going to the magic lantern show without her permission."

"I'm not sure that Uncle Roger meant what he said," remarked the Story Girl. "I couldn't get a look into his eyes. They usually twinkle when he is teasing us. He can never help that. You know he would think it a great joke to frighten us like this. It's really dreadful to have no grown-ups you can depend upon."

"We could depend on Father if he were here," said Dan firmly. "He'd tell us the truth."

"He would tell us what he *thought* was true, Dan, but he couldn't *know*. He's not as well educated as the editor of the *Enterprise*. No, there's nothing to do but wait and see," I answered.

"Let's go into the house and read what the Bible says about it," suggested Cecily.

We crept in carefully, lest we disturb Aunt Olivia. Cecily found and read the portion of Scripture that told about the coming judgment of God. We found some comfort in it.

"Well," said the Story Girl finally. "I must go and get the potatoes ready. I suppose they must be boiled even if it is Judgment Day tomorrow. But I don't believe it."

"And I've got to go and plant elderberries," said Peter. "I don't see how I can do it—go way back there alone. I'll feel scared to death the whole time."

"Tell Uncle Roger that. And say that if tomorrow is the end of the world, there is no good in planting any more fields," I suggested.

"Yes, and if he lets you off, then we'll know he was in earnest," chimed in Cecily. "But if he still says you must go, that'll be a sign that he doesn't believe it."

The rest of us went home, leaving the Story Girl and Peter to do their work. Aunt Janet had found the old broken blue cup and gave poor Felicity a bitter scolding about it. But Felicity didn't seem to mind.

"Ma can't believe tomorrow is the last day. If she did, she wouldn't scold like that," she told us. This comforted us until after dinner when the Story Girl and Peter came over and told us that Uncle Roger had gone to Summerside, just as he had told us he planned to do. We were plunged into fear again.

"Uncle Roger said I had to plant the elderberries just the same," said Peter. "He said it might not be Judgment Day tomorrow, though he believed it was. He said it would keep me out of mischief. But I just can't stand it back there alone. Some of you fellows must come with me. I don't mean for you to do my work but only to keep me company."

It was finally decided that Dan and Felix should go. I wanted to go also, but the girls protested.

"You must stay and keep us cheered up," begged Felicity. "I don't know how I'm going to spend the afternoon. I promised Kitty Marr that I'd go down and see her, but I can't now. And I can't knit my lace either. I'd just keep thinking, *What's the use? Perhaps it will all be burned up tomorrow.*"

So I stayed with the girls and we had a miserable afternoon. The Story Girl declared again and again that she "didn't believe it." But when we asked her to tell a story, she refused, offering a few flimsy excuses.

Cecily pestered the life out of Aunt Janet, asking repeatedly, "Ma, will you be washing Monday?" or "Ma, will you be going to prayer meeting Tuesday night?" or "Ma, will you be picking raspberries next week?" It was a great comfort to her each time her mother said "yes" or "of course," as if there were no question about it.

Sara Ray cried until I wondered how one small head could contain all the tears she shed. I don't think she was as much frightened as disappointed that she had no white dress. In midafternoon, Cecily came downstairs with her forget-me-not jug in her hand. This was a dainty piece of china, which Cecily loved. She always kept her toothbrush in it.

"Sara, I want to give you this jug," she said seriously.

Sara had always liked the jug. She stopped crying long enough to take it happily.

"Oh, Cecily, thank you. But are you sure you won't want it back if tomorrow isn't Judgment Day?"

"No, it's yours for good," she said in a resigned voice.

"Are you going to give anyone your cherry vase?" asked Felicity, trying to sound indifferent. Felicity had always admired the cherry vase Aunt Olivia had given to Cecily one Christmas.

"No, I'm not," said Cecily quickly.

"Oh, well *I* don't care," answered Felicity. "Only if tomorrow is the last day, the cherry vase won't be of much use to you."

"I guess it will do me as much good as anyone else," said Cecily indignantly. She was not about to give her prized vase to Felicity. Giving her jug to the pitiful Sara Ray was one thing. But she had no special warmth for Felicity.

At dusk, the fears that clutched us became worse. We could hear Aunt Janet telling Aunt Olivia about it and laughing at us. Aunt Olivia seemed quite recovered from her headache and getting a real kick out of the fact that we thought the end of the world was coming.

"Perhaps they won't be laughing so hard tomorrow," said Dan gloomily.

We were sitting on the steps, watching what might be our last sunset on the dark hills. Peter was with us. It was his Sunday to go home, but he decided to stay and be with us.

"If tomorrow is Judgment Day, I want to be with all of you," he said.

Sara Ray had wanted to stay also, but her mother told her she must be home before dark.

"Never mind, Sara," comforted Cecily. "Judgment Day isn't supposed to begin until tomorrow at two o'clock."

"I'm sure I won't sleep a wink tonight," said Felix.

"I wonder where we'll all be this time tomorrow night," I said as we watched the sunset deepen to shades of purple and fiery red.

"I'm going to read the Bible all afternoon tomorrow," Peter said.

Aunt Olivia came out for an evening walk, looking very lovely in a pretty summer dress and swinging her hat on her arm. She smiled a friendly smile at all of us. We all loved Aunt Olivia. But just now we resented her and Aunt Janet for laughing at us, so we refused to smile back.

"What a sulky, sulky lot of little people," Aunt Olivia said, going across the yard, holding her dress up from the dewy grass.

Peter decided to stay all night with us. When we went to bed, it was a dark stormy night. The rain was crying on the roof as if the whole world were weeping because its end was so near.

No one forgot or hurried his or her prayers that night. We would have loved to have left the candle burning, but Aunt Janet wouldn't allow it. So we blew it out and lay there quaking and shivering, with the wild rain streaming down the window. The voice of the storm wailed all night long as we lay listening—for what? We didn't know.

Judgment Day

We watched and waited nervously. The moments dragged by, each seeming to last an hour. Would two o'clock never come? We all became very nervous. Even Peter stopped reading. Any unusual sound made us jump. Could it be the last trumpet?

Chapter Six

Sunday morning came, dull and gray. The rain had stopped, but the clouds hung dark and angry above the world. It seemed like a perfect morning for Judgment Day. We were all up early. None of us had slept well, and some of us had not slept at all. We were surprised that the Story Girl had not slept. She always was so cool and on top of things. But this morning she looked very pale and had black shadows under her eyes.

Peter slept better than any of us after all his hard work planting elderberries. "It would have taken more than Judgment Day to keep me awake after working so hard yesterday," he grumped. "But at least I was busy, so I couldn't think too much. When I woke up, though, I was worse scared than ever."

Cecily was pale but brave. For the first time in years, she had not put her hair up in curlers on Saturday night. It was brushed and braided, and she looked like a little pilgrim.

"If it's Judgment Day, I don't care whether my hair is curly or not," she said.

"Well," Aunt Janet said as we trooped into the kitchen, "this is the first time you kids ever all got up without being called."

At breakfast our appetites were poor. How could the grown-ups eat as they did? After breakfast, we did our chores. We didn't know how we would make it through the rest of the day until two o'clock. Peter got out his Bible and began to read from the first chapter in Genesis.

"I won't have time to read it all through, I s'pose," he said, "but I'll read as fast as I can."

We had a circuit-riding preacher who came every other week to our church in Carlisle, but this was not his week to come. So no one preached in Carlisle that day, and Sunday school was held in the evening. Cecily got out her lesson and studied it even though we all feared the end would come before we had our Sunday school that night.

"If it isn't Judgment Day today, I want to have the lesson learned anyway," she said. "We know Judgment Day will come sometime. When it does come, I'll feel I've done what was right."

The hours dragged on. We roamed around the house and yard trying to keep busy and forget our fears—all but Peter, who was still reading his Bible. By eleven o'clock he had read through Genesis and was starting on Exodus.

"There's a bunch of stuff in here that I don't understand," he said, "but I read every word, and that's the main thing. That story about Joseph and his brothers was so in'tresting that I almost forgot about the Judgment Day."

The long drawn-out dread about the coming Judgment was beginning to get on Dan's nerves.

"If it *is* Judgment Day," he growled, "I wish it would hurry up and get over with."

"Oh Dan!" cried Felicity and Cecily together in horror. But the Story Girl looked as if she rather sympathized with Dan.

If we had eaten little at breakfast, we ate less at lunch. After lunch the clouds rolled away, and the sun came out gloriously. We thought this was a good sign. Felicity said she didn't think it would have cleared up so nicely if it were Judgment Day. Nevertheless, we dressed ourselves carefully, and the girls put on their white dresses.

Sara Ray came up—still crying, of course. She made us more afraid by saying that her mother believed the article in the newspaper and thought the end of the world was really coming.

"That's why she let me come up," she sobbed. "If she hadn't been afraid, I don't believe she would have let me come today. But I'd have died if I couldn't have. And she wasn't a bit cross when I told her I had gone to the magic lantern show. That's an awful bad sign, don't you think? I don't have a white dress, but I put on my best white apron with the ruffles."

"That's unusual, Sara," said Felicity in her uppity way. "You wouldn't put on an apron to go to church. It doesn't seem proper to put on one for Judgment Day either."

"It's the best I could do," said Sara tearfully. "I wanted to wear something white. It's just like a white dress without sleeves."

"It's lovely, Sara," said the Story Girl. "Just lovely—and besides, God doesn't look on the outside. He looks at your heart.

"Let's go to the orchard to wait," she continued. "It's one o'clock now, so in another hour we'll know the worst. We'll leave the front door open to the house, so we'll hear the big clock when it strikes two."

It seemed like a good plan. It was too wet to sit on the grass, so we sat on the low branches of one of the "climbing" trees. The world was beautiful, peaceful, and green. Above us, there was a dazzling blue sky spotted with heaps of white clouds.

"Aw fudge!" said Dan, beginning to whistle bravely. "I don't believe there's any chance of it being the last day."

"Dan! You aren't supposed to whistle on Sunday," warned Felicity severely. Sometimes she really made us tired with all her rules—they were mostly made-up ones.

"I'm almost all the way through Exodus, and I don't see anything about whistling on Sunday," Peter remarked. He had his Bible open and was still reading.

"I don't see anything about Methodists or Presbyterians either. When does it tell about them?" he asked seriously.

"There's nothing about Methodists or Presbyterians in the Bible," answered Felicity.

Peter looked amazed. "Well, how did they happen then?" he asked. "How did they begin?"

"I've often thought it such a strange thing that there isn't a word about either of them in the Bible," said Cecily. "It does mention Baptists—John the Baptist, you know."

Some of us didn't *know* but we acted like we did.

"Well, even if it isn't Judgment Day, I'm going to keep on reading the Bible until I get clear through it. I never knew it was such an in'tresting book," Peter concluded.

"You shouldn't call it an *interesting* book," said Felicity, again in a know-it-all way. "Why, you might be talking about just *any* book."

"I didn't mean any harm," said Peter defensively.

"The Bible *is* an interesting book," said the Story Girl, coming to Peter's rescue. "There are magnificent stories in it—yes, Felicity, *magnificent*. If the world doesn't come to an end today, I'll tell you the story of Ruth next Sunday. I'll tell it anyhow—no matter where we are. That's a promise. Wherever we are next Sunday, I'll tell you about Ruth."

"You wouldn't tell stories in heaven, would you?" asked Cecily timidly.

"Why not?" replied the Story Girl with a flash of her eyes. "Indeed I will. I'll tell stories as long as I've a tongue to talk and someone to listen."

We were sure she would. Even the angels might stop their harping to listen to some tale she would tell about the mortals on earth. Somehow this thought comforted us. We wouldn't fear the Judgment so much if somehow we could keep our own personalities in heaven.

"It must be getting near two o'clock," said Cecily fearfully.

We watched and waited nervously. The moments dragged by, each seeming to last an hour. Would two o'clock never come? We all became very nervous. Even Peter stopped reading. Any unusual sound made us jump. Could it be the last trumpet? A cloud passed over the sun. As the shadow passed over the orchard, we trembled. A wagon rumbling over the plank bridge on the road caused Sara Ray to let out a scream. And the slamming of the barn door over at Uncle Roger's farm next door caused us to break out in a cold sweat.

"I don't believe it's Judgment Day," said my brother Felix. "But I wish that clock would strike two."

"Can't you tell us a story to pass the time?" I begged the Story Girl.

She shook her head. "No, it would be no use to try. But if this isn't Judgment Day, I'll have a great story to tell about us being so scared," she smiled.

Paddy, her cat, came running into the orchard, proudly carrying a big field mouse, which he dropped in front of us like a trophy. He sat right there and began to eat it—body, bones, and all, licking his chops with gusto.

"If that clock doesn't strike soon, I will go out of my mind," declared Cecily.

"Time always seems long when you're waiting," said the Story Girl. "But it does seem as if we've been here longer than an hour."

"Maybe the clock struck, and we didn't hear it," suggested Dan. "Maybe we ought to check and see if it did."

Cecily volunteered. "I suppose if anything happens, I'll have time to get back to you," she said, jumping up to go to the house.

We watched her go through the gate in her white dress. A few minutes passed—or a few years. We could not have told which. Then Cecily came running at full speed back to us. But when she reached us, she was trembling so hard that at first she couldn't speak.

"What is it? Is it past two?" begged the Story Girl.

"It's . . . it's four," said Cecily with a gasp. "The old clock isn't going. Mother forgot to wind it up last night, and it stopped. But it's four o'clock by the kitchen clock, so it isn't Judgment Day!" We began to breathe again as we saw our lives and our futures spared.

"Mother has tea ready, and she says to come in."

Just like that, our morbid fear and dread lifted.

"I'll never believe anything I read in the newspaper again," said Dan.

"I told you the Bible was more to be depended on than the newspapers," said Cecily proudly.

Sara Ray and the Story Girl went home, and we went in to tea with huge appetites. Afterward, as we dressed for Sunday school, we let off steam, laughing and hollering with such joy and relief that Aunt Janet had to come up to settle us down.

"Children, have you forgotten today is Sunday?" she reminded us. We were always supposed to be quieter on Sunday in respect for the Lord's Day.

As we walked down the hill to church, Felix remarked, "Isn't it great that we have more time to live in this nice world?"

"It sure did make me think about it all, though," replied Peter. "I wish I hadn't been so quick to decide to be a Presbyterian."

"Well, now you have time to change your mind," said Dan.

"Not on your life. I ain't that kind of a guy. Once I decide, that's it!" answered Peter. "Presbyterian it will be."

"I wish I hadn't been so quick to give away my forget-me-not jug," said Cecily wistfully.

"That's not as big a deal as being a Presbyterian for life," answered Peter. "But I guess that don't matter none either. You said before that what's really important is being a Christian. Didn't you say you had a story about Presbyterians? Tell us. You've got time before we get to church."

The Story Girl began as we walked along. "Long ago when Judy Pineau was young, she was hired as a maid to Elder Frewen's wife. Mrs. Frewen had been a schoolteacher and was very particular about how people talked and the grammar they used. She wanted people to use *refined* words.

"One very hot day she heard Judy Pineau say she was 'all in a sweat.' Mrs. Frewen was greatly shocked. 'Judy, you shouldn't say *sweat*,' she said. 'Horses *sweat*. You should say you are "in a *perspiration*."'

"Well, Judy said she would try to remember, because she liked Mrs. Frewen and wanted to please her. Not long after that, Judy was scrubbing the kitchen floor one morning when Mrs. Frewen came in. Judy looked up and said, quite proud that she had used the right word, 'Oh, Mees Frewen, ain't it awful hot? I do declare I'm all in a *Presbyterian.*'"

"I guess that's me, all right," laughed Peter. "I'm *all* in a *Presbyterian* for *life,*" he added. And he was.

Dreamer of Dreams

"Maybe that pink cloud is a dream getting all ready to float down into somebody's sleep," suggested the Story Girl.

Chapter Seven

August went out and September came in. Harvest was ended, and summer was fading fast. A faint blue smoke hung over the hills and valleys, and we could tell fall was on the way. The apples were burnt red and hanging low on the branches. Crickets sang day and night, and squirrels chattered away, telling each other secrets. The sunshine was thick and yellow as gold. School opened, and the days were growing shorter. The nights were lovely, watched over by the autumn stars. It was still warm during the day, but the nights had a chilly nip to them. It was perfect sleeping weather.

We were sitting in a circle around the Pulpit Stone writing memories in our journals. All of us were eating the Reverend Mr. Scott's plums, which in September had turned ripe and juicy in their blue skins. The Reverend Mr. Scott was dead and gone, but the plums from his tree kept his memory alive much better than his forgotten sermons.

"I would really like to know what special kind of devilry you kids are up to this time," said Uncle Roger as he passed through the orchard going hunting.

"Oh," said Felicity in a shocked tone when he passed by. "Uncle Roger *swore*."

"No, he didn't," said the Story Girl quickly. "'Devilry' isn't swearing at all. It only means extra-bad mischief."

"Well, it's not a very nice word, anyhow," said Felicity.

"No, it isn't," agreed the Story Girl with a sigh. "It's very expressive, but it isn't nice. That is the way with so many words. They're expressive, but they're not nice, so a girl can't use them."

The Story Girl loved expressive words and treasured them as some girls might treasure pearls. To her they were like lustrous pearls, threaded on a golden cord of vivid fancy. When she met with a new one, she uttered it over and over to herself, loving and caressing it until she had made it her own.

"Well, anyhow it isn't a suitable word in this case," insisted Felicity. "We are not up to any dev— any extra-bad mischief at all."

And we weren't. Not even the strictest grown-up could call what we were doing devilry. We were simply writing down our memories of the summer. We had been at it every day for weeks. During that time each day, we all wrote in our journals. The Story Girl had suggested it one rainy evening when we could find nothing to do.

We had been picking a good supply of spruce gum until the rain interrupted us. The Story Girl suggested that each of us make a *Summer Journal of Memories*. It was a great idea, and if anything, it was keeping us *out* of mischief.

All of us had big wads of the spruce gum in our mouths, which we were chewing loudly as we wrote.

"My aunt Jane says it isn't polite to chew gum anywhere," remarked Peter.

"I don't suppose your aunt Jane knew *all* the rules of etiquette," said Felicity nastily, trying to crush Peter.

But Peter was not to be crushed. He had a certain toughness that was incredible.

"She did too," he retorted. "My aunt Jane was a real lady, even if she was only a Craig. She knew all those rules, and she kept them when there was nobody around to see. And she was smart! If Father only had half of her git-up-and-git, he wouldn't of been a drinker. And I wouldn't be a hired boy today."

"Have you any idea where your father is?" asked Dan.

"No," said Peter. "The last we heard of him, he was a lumberjack in the Maine woods. But that was

three years ago. I don't know where he is now."
Taking his gum from his mouth to make his statement
more impressive, he added, "And I don't care!"

"Oh, Peter, that sounds dreadful," said Cecily.
"Your own father!"

"Well," said Peter defiantly, "if your own father
ran away when you was a baby and left your mother
to earn her living by washing and working for folks,
I guess you wouldn't care much about him either."

"What if your father comes home one of these
days with a huge fortune," suggested the Story Girl.

"Perhaps pigs can whistle, but it isn't likely," was
all the answer he gave to this suggestion.

"There goes Mr. Campbell down the road," said
Dan.

"That's his new mare. Isn't she a dandy? Her
skin is like black satin. He calls her Betty Sherman."

"I don't think it's very nice to call a horse the same
name as your grandmother," said Felicity.

"Betty Sherman would have thought it a compliment," said the Story Girl.

Betty Sherman, a real-life character whom the
Story Girl had told us about, was a legend on Prince
Edward Island. She was a beauty who had become
famous by proposing to the man she loved.

"Maybe Betty Sherman would want a horse
named after her, but *not me*," said Felicity with

mphasis. "She couldn't have been very nice, or he would never have gone and asked a man to marry her."

"Why not?" asked Sara Stanley, our Story Girl.

"Goodness me, that's dreadful! Would *you* do such a thing yourself?"

"I don't know," said the Story Girl, laughing. "If I wanted him *dreadfully*, and *he* wouldn't do the asking, perhaps I would."

"I'd forty times rather die an old maid," exclaimed Felicity.

"Nobody as pretty as you will ever be an old maid, Felicity," said Peter, looking at her with stars in his eyes.

Felicity tried to look angry with Peter, but it didn't fool us at all. We knew she liked his compliment. Even though Peter was just a hired boy, he was a handsome one and well liked by us all. Felicity's pride was enormous, but we all thought she secretly liked Peter, no matter how hard she tried to hide the fact.

"It wouldn't be ladylike to ask anyone to marry you," said our sweet Cecily sincerely.

"I suppose that old girl's magazine, *Family Guide,* would think so too," agreed the Story Girl with sarcasm in her voice. The Story Girl had never thought much of the *Family Guide* the way the other girls had. They read the etiquette column every week that told them just what kind of gloves should be worn at a wedding or what they should say to introduce someone. It even told them how they ought to *look* when their best young men came to see them. What a pain!

"They say Mrs. Richard Cook asked *her* husband to marry *her*," said Dan.

"Uncle Roger says that she didn't exactly ask him, but she was so slick that Richard was engaged before he knew what hit him," said the Story Girl. "I know a story about Mrs. Cook's grandmother. She was one of those women who is always saying, 'I told you so.'"

"Take notice, Felicity," said Dan. She made a face at him.

"Anyway, Mrs. Cook was very stubborn," continued the Story Girl. "Soon after they were married, she and her husband quarreled about an apple tree. They couldn't remember for sure what kind of apple tree it was. She said it was a Yellow Transparent tree, and he said it was a Golden Delicious. This was before there was a *Family Guide* magazine to tell men it isn't polite to say shut up to their wives, so he did. She didn't speak to him for five years. Can you believe it? She didn't speak a word to him for *five years*. In five years' time, the tree bore apples and they *were* Yellow Transparent. And then she spoke at last. She said, 'I told you so!'"

"And did she talk to him after that as usual?" asked Sara Ray.

"Oh, yes, she was just the same as she had been before," said the Story Girl. "But that isn't part of the story. It stops when she spoke at last. You're never satisfied to leave a story where it should stop, Sara Ray."

"I always like to know what happened afterward," answered Sara Ray.

"Uncle Roger says he wouldn't want a wife he could never quarrel with," remarked Dan. "He says it would be too tame a life for him."

"I wonder if Uncle Roger will always stay a bachelor since he won't take anyone," said Cecily.

"He seems real happy," observed Peter.

"Ma says that it's all right for now that he is a bachelor because he doesn't want a wife, but when he gets old he'll be sorry. He won't have anyone to take care of him then."

"If your aunt Olivia got married, what would your uncle Roger do for a housekeeper?" asked Peter.

"Oh, Aunt Olivia will never be married now. She's way too old," said the all-wise Felicity. "Why, she'll be twenty-nine in January, you know."

"I'm not sure about that," argued Peter. "She's awful pretty, so she might find someone yet."

"Wouldn't it be exciting to have a wedding in the family?" smiled Cecily. "I've been to four funerals but never to a wedding."

"I've never even been to a funeral," said Sara Ray gloomily. She acted like she had been really deprived.

"There's the Wedding Veil of the Proud Princess," cried Cecily, pointing to a long drift of cloudlike smoke. "I'll never forget that story Sara Stanley told us. Look at the sweet pink cloud below it."

"Maybe that pink cloud is a dream getting all ready to float down into somebody's sleep," suggested the Story Girl.

"I had a perfectly awful dream last night," said Cecily, with a shudder as she remembered it. "I dreamed I was on a desert island with tigers and natives who had two heads."

"Cecily," said the Story Girl in rebuke, "why couldn't you tell it better than that? If I had had such a dream, I would tell it so that everybody else would feel as if they had dreamed it too."

"Well, I'm not you," answered Cecily, "and I wouldn't want to frighten anyone like I was frightened. It was an awful dream but kind of interesting too."

"I've had some real in'tresting dreams," said Peter, "but I can't remember them long. I wish I could."

"Why don't you write them down?" suggested the Story Girl. "I have an idea. Let's all get notebooks like our memory journals and call them our dream journals. We can write down all of our dreams, just as we dream them. We'll see who has the most interesting one. And we'll have them to read when we're old and gray."

Instantly we all saw ourselves old and gray—all but the Story Girl. We could not picture her as old. Always, it seemed she would have sleek brown curls, a voice like the sound of a harp string in the wind, and eyes like the stars of eternal youth.

The Dream Books

"I hate to dream of being chased because
I can never run," said Sara Ray with a
shiver. "I just stand there rooted to the
ground. I see whatever it is coming, but
I can't move. I sure hope I never dream
Peg Bowen chases me. I'll die if I do."

Chapter Eight

The next day, the Story Girl coaxed Uncle Roger to take her to Markdale. There she bought our dream books. They were ten cents apiece, with ruled pages and green covers. My own lies open beside me as I write. Its pages, now yellow with age, contain descriptions of the dreams that haunted my childhood slumbers on those nights long ago.

As I turn the pages and glance over the childish records—each one beginning, "Last night I dreamed"—the past comes back vividly to me. I see that orchard in full bloom, shining in my memory, where we sat on those September evenings and wrote down our dreams. Felix, Peter, Dan, Cecily, Felicity, Sara Ray, and the Story Girl are all around me once more. I see us sitting in the sweet-smelling grass, each with an open dream book and a pencil in hand, writing busily. I see us pausing, thinking, and trying to find a suitable word. I hear their laughing voices and see their bright, unclouded eyes. In this little old book, filled with cramped boyish writing, there is a spell of magic that brings me back to those delightful days.

Beverley King is a boy once more, writing down his dreams in the old King orchard on the homestead hill, blown over by the end-of-summer winds. Opposite me sits the Story Girl, her beautiful bare feet crossed, one slender hand on her knee, propping her head as she thinks of how to write some wonderful dream story.

There to the right is sweet Cecily, with the dark brown eyes, a fat little dictionary beside her. You can't be expected to know how to spell every word of your dreams, especially when you are just eleven.

Next to her sits Felicity—beautiful, and conscious that she is beautiful, with hair of spun gold, sea-blue eyes, and roses in her cheeks.

Peter, beside her, of course, is sprawled flat on his stomach in the grass. He is finding it is harder work to write than to hoe a field. His terrible spelling, even with Cecily's dictionary, is a curious wonder. The Story Girl will go over his dreams when he has finished and put in the commas and punctuation and straighten out the spelling.

Felix sits on the right side of the Story Girl, plump and stodgy, grimly serious even over dreams. He writes with his knees stuck up to form a writing desk, and he frowns fiercely the whole time.

Dan, like Peter, lies on the ground, digging his toes into the soft grass. All the while he writes, he groans when he cannot find the word to suit him.

Sara Ray is at his left. What can be said of her, except to tell where she sits? Bless her heart; her dream book is just as colorless as she is.

Each of us was very anxious to have the most exciting dream book. But we were an honorable little crew, and I don't think we ever wrote anything down that had not really been dreamed. At first we thought the Story Girl's dream book would be the best, but hers was no more remarkable than any of the others. Cecily seemed to have the most dramatic dreams. She, the meekest and mildest of us all, was in the habit of dreaming the most terrible things. Almost every night, battle, murder, or sudden death played some part in her colorful slumber.

On the other hand, Dan, who lived on the edge and read dime novels, that he borrowed from other boys at school, dreamed dreams of a quiet and peaceful kind. He was quite disgusted with the tame results in his dream book.

If the Story Girl's dreams were no better than ours, she at least scored higher when it came to re-telling them. To hear her tell a dream was as good (or as bad) as dreaming it yourself.

As far as writing them down was concerned, I, Beverley King, carried the prize. I had a good reputation for writing and composition. But the Story Girl was even better than I. She had inherited some of her artistic father's talent and *illustrated* her dreams with sketches that caught the spirit of them.

The Story Girl had a special knack for drawing monsters. I vividly recall a hideous picture of a huge reptile-like dinosaur that sent Sara Ray into a crying fit. Another time the Story Girl told a dream of being chased around by the ottoman (a stuffed parlor stool). The grimacing monster ottoman in her dream book made Sara Ray so fearful she ran home wailing, imagining she was being chased by every piece of furniture she saw. What a girl!

Sara Ray's dreams never amounted to much. She was always in trouble of some sort—couldn't get her hair braided or her shoes on the right feet. The only thing worth mentioning was the one where she dreamed she went for a ride in a hot-air balloon and fell out.

"I expected to come down with an awful thud," she said shuddering. "But I lit as light as a feather and woke right up."

"I dreamed last night that I threw a lighted match into a keg of gunpowder in Mr. Cook's store at Markdale," said Peter. "Everything blew up, and they fished me out of the mess. But I woke up before I found out if I was killed or not."

"That's always a problem," said Story Girl sadly. "I usually wake up just as things are getting interesting."

"I dreamed last night that I really had curly hair," complained Cecily. "Oh, I was so happy! It was dreadful to wake up and find it as straight as ever."

Felix had a sick spell soon after we began our dream books. Aunt Janet wanted to try to cure him by giving him a dose of liver pills, which Elder Frewen said was a cure-all for every disease. But Felix refused to take the liver pills. He said he was afraid to take them because he had heard someone say they had taken liver pills and never dreamed again.

"I'd rather be sick than take liver pills and not dream anymore. I want to have lots of dreams to put in my book," he said firmly.

"That's silly, Felix. You don't know that's why that other person never dreamed again," said Cecily. "I guess you'll just have to get over your sickness without any medicine."

"I had an exciting dream last night," said Dan. "I dreamed old Peg Bowen chased me. I saw myself up at her house and she took after me. You bet I scooted. But she caught me. I felt her skinny hand reach out and clutch my shoulder. I let out a screech and woke right up."

"You sure did screech," said Felicity. "We heard you clear over in our room."

"I hate to dream of being chased because I can never run," said Sara Ray with a shiver. "I just stand there rooted to the ground. I see whatever it is coming, but I can't move. I sure hope I never dream Peg Bowen chases me. I'll die if I do."

"I wonder what Peg Bowen would do to a fellow if she caught him?" questioned Dan.

"Peg Bowen don't need to catch you to do things to you. She can just look at you and bad things happen," Peter said.

"I don't believe that," said the Story Girl. "She's just an old lady people have told stories about."

"Well, last summer she paid a visit to Lem Hill's farm in Markdale. He told her to get out or he'd set the dog on her. Peg cleared out, cutting across his pasture. As she went, she was muttering stuff under her breath. The next day his best cow died."

"It might have happened anyhow," said the Story Girl, but she didn't seem to have as much confidence as she had before.

"It might have," agreed Peter. "But I'd just as soon Peg Bowen didn't look at *my* cows."

"As if you had any cows!" giggled Felicity.

"I'm going to have cows someday," said Peter with a flushed red face. "I don't mean to be a hired boy all of my life. I'll have a farm of my own and cows . . . and . . . everything. You'll see."

"I dreamed last night that Felix was thin," said Peter laughing. He looked so strange. His clothes just hung loose, and he was going round trying to hold them up." Everybody thought this was funny except Felix. He wouldn't speak to Peter for two days because of it.

Felicity also got into trouble because of her dreams. One night she woke up from a very exciting dream. She was able to go back to sleep again, but the next morning she couldn't remember the dream at all. She determined she would never let another dream get away from her like that. So the next time she awoke from a dream, she got right up and began to write it down. While doing so, she accidentally set fire to her nightgown with the candle—a brand-new gown trimmed with lots and lots of lace. She burned a huge hole in it, and when Aunt Janet discovered it, she gave her a severe scolding. Felicity was used to her mother's sharp tongue, which may have been part of the reason she was so sharp-tongued herself. Her comment was, "Anyhow, I saved my dream."

That, of course, seemed to be the only thing that mattered. It is true that money can buy a lot of things, but you cannot buy back a dream. When I consider all of the dreams of my childhood, the one that has been fulfilled is that I still have a fun relationship with my cousins. It began that summer on the farm at Prince Edward Island. This old dream book I have here in my hand brings back the happy memories of those days—and to return there is one of the great delights of my life. Although the years have flown by, we are still the King cousins of Avonlea. That identity will always bring me joy.

Lucy Maud Montgomery
1908

Lucy Maud Montgomery
1874-1942

Anne of Green Gables was the very first book that Lucy Maud Montgomery published. In all, she wrote twenty-five books.

Lucy Maud Montgomery was born on Prince Edward Island. Her family called her Maud. Before she was two years old, her mother died and she was sent to live with her mother's parents on their farm on the Island. Her grandparents were elderly and very strict. Maud lived with them for a long time.

When she was seven, her father remarried. He moved far out west to Saskatchewan, Canada, with his new wife. At age seventeen, she went to live with them, but she did not get along with her stepmother. So she returned to her grandparents.

She attended college and studied to become a teacher—just like Anne in the Avonlea series. When her grandfather died, Maud went home to be with her grandmother. Living there in the quiet of Prince Edward Island, she had plenty of time to write. It was during this time that she wrote her first book, *Anne of Green Gables*. When the book was finally accepted, it was published soon after. It was an immediate hit, and Maud began to get thousands of letters asking for more stories about Anne. She wrote *Anne of Avonlea, Chronicles of Avonlea, Anne of the Island, Anne of Windy Poplars, Anne's House of Dreams, Rainbow Valley, Anne of Ingleside*, and *Rilla of Ingleside*. She also wrote *The Story Girl* and *The Golden Road*.

When Maud was thirty-seven years old, Ewan Macdonald, the minister of the local Presbyterian Church in Canvendish, proposed marriage to her. Maud accepted and they were married. Later on they moved to Ontario where two sons, Chester and Stewart, were born to the couple.

Maud never went back to Prince Edward Island to live again. But when she died in 1942, she was buried on the Island, near the house known as Green Gables.

Excerpt from

The Story Girl

Book 4

DREAMS, SCHEMES, AND MYSTERIES

NOW AVAILABLE

"I've thought of a splendid plan," she said. "It flashed into my mind when the uncles were talking about Uncle Edward. The beauty of it is that we can play it on Sundays. You know there are so few things we are allowed to do on Sundays, but this is a Christian game, so it will be all right."

"It isn't like the religious fruit basket game, is it?" asked Cecily anxiously. This was a game that hadn't worked out for us because of Peter. He couldn't play because he didn't know the Scriptures very well.

"No, this isn't a game at all," said the Story Girl. "It is this: Each of you boys must preach a sermon like Uncle Edward used to. Each of you choose a Sunday to preach, and we girls will judge which sermon is best and give you a prize. I'll give that picture that Father sent me last week."

The picture was a famous artist's picture of a fine deer. We boys were pleased and agreed. It was decided that I would be the first one to preach. I lay awake for an hour that night, thinking about what Scripture text I should use for the following Sunday. After tea the next day, I went to the barn and sat on a bale of hay, writing what I hoped would be a masterpiece of a sermon.

I decided to preach on missions. Using words, I painted a terrible picture of the dark, awful life of the poor heathen who bowed down to gods of wood and stone. God's who could never help them. Each time I had an important point to make, I wrote the word "thump" in red ink, so I'd be sure to thump the pulpit to emphasize the point.

I still have that sermon with all its unfaded red "thumps." It is filed away with my dream book. I'm not as proud of it as I once was. At the time, I didn't think Felix could beat it. And I certainly didn't think Dan had a chance—he wasn't even religious. As for Peter, I didn't suppose a boy who had hardly gone to church in his life could even be in the running to compete with me. He had so little education, and I came from a family with a real minister in it. Surely, I thought, I had the best chance of all to win that picture.

I wanted to memorize my sermon, so I preached it over and over with only Paddy sitting in the audience in the barn, patiently listening.

When we went to church the next Sunday, Reverend Marwood, the pastor, had at least three interested listeners. Felix, Peter, and I were taking mental notes on the art of preaching. Not a motion or a word escaped us. To be sure, none of us could even remember the text when we got home. But we knew just how to throw our heads back and clutch the edges of the pulpit when we announced it.

In the afternoon we all went to the orchard with our Bibles and hymnbooks in hand. I went up the stone steps of the Pulpit Stone, feeling rather nervous. My audience sat down gravely on the grass in front of me. We began with singing and the reading of the Scripture. We had agreed to omit the prayer, as that seemed too serious for playacting. But we took up a collection for missions. Dan passed one of Felicity's rosebud plates, and everyone put in a penny.

Before I was halfway through my sermon, I realized that it was horrible. It seemed to me that I preached it well enough. I didn't forget one thump. But my audience was plainly bored. When I stepped down from the pulpit, I felt I had failed to make any impression at all. Felix would be sure to get the prize.

"That was a very good sermon for a first attempt," the Story Girl said graciously. "It sounded just like real sermons I have heard."

At first she made me feel that I had not done so badly after all. But the other girls weighed in with their comments and my hopes were dashed.

"Every word of it was true," said Cecily, as though trying to say something good about it.

"I often feel," said Felicity in her prim, stuck-up way, "that we don't think enough about the heathen. Your sermon made me at least *think* about them."

Sara Ray really put me in my place. "I liked it 'cause it was nice and short," she said.

Later I asked Dan what he thought of it. Since he had decided not to compete, I thought I could depend on him for the truth.

"It was too much like a regular sermon to be interesting," said Dan frankly.

"I'd think that's what it should have been," I replied.

"Not if you wanted to make an impression," said Dan seriously. "You needed to have something different for that. Now Peter, he'll have something different."

"I don't think Peter can preach a sermon. He's hardly even gone to church," I replied.

"Maybe not," Dan answered, "but you'll see. He'll make an impression."

Peter's turn came next. He didn't write his sermon out. "That's too much hard work," he said.

"And I ain't choosing a text or a special Scripture verse for the whole sermon."

"Whoever heard of a sermon without a text?" asked Felix.

"I'm going to have a subject instead of a text. It will have three headings. You didn't have a single heading, Bev," he said to me. "If you have headings, you won't wander all over the Bible. You'll be more organized."

I was sorry I hadn't had headings and figured I would have made more of an impression if I had used some. "How's one to know about headings?" I asked.

"Well, I'm going to have them," said Peter.

"What are you going to preach on?" asked Felix.

"You'll find out next Sunday," Peter said, and that was all he would say.

The next Sunday was the first of October—a lovely day, as warm as June. We sat around the Pulpit Stone and waited for Peter. It was his Sunday off, and he had gone home the night before, but he said he'd be back for sure to preach his sermon. Soon he arrived. I felt right away that he had the advantage over me because he looked so handsome in his new navy blue suit, white collar, and bow tie. His black eyes shone and his curls were brushed up so that he sure looked the part of a minister.

Sara Ray was late but we decided to go ahead. We never knew for sure when she was coming. Sometimes her mother would change her plans at the last minute.

Peter chose the hymn we would sing and read the chapter of Scripture as if he'd been doing it all of his life. Reverend Marwood himself couldn't have done better.

"We will sing the hymn, omitting the fourth stanza," Peter said.

That was a fine touch that I had not thought of. I began to think Peter might have a chance to win after all.

When Peter was ready to begin, he put his hands in his pockets—something not usually done by ministers—and plunged in. He spoke in a conversational tone. He didn't put on a minister voice. He made his sermon very believable. There was no one writing it down, but I could have preached it again, word for word. And so could everyone else who heard it. It was an unforgettable sermon.

"Dearly beloved," said Peter, "my sermon is about the bad place—in short—hell."

An electric shock seemed to run through all of us listening. Everyone suddenly looked alert. Peter had in one sentence done what my whole sermon had failed to do. He had made an impression.

The King Cousins
(Book 1)
By L.M. Montgomery,
Adapted by Barbara Davoll

Sara Stanley, the Story Girl, can captivate any-one who will listen to her tales. In this first book of the series, brothers Beverley and Felix arrive on Prince Edward Island to spend the summer with their cousins on the King homestead. These curious and imaginative children set out to investigate the existence of God.

SOFTCOVER 0-310-70598-3

Available now at your local bookstore!

Zonder**kidz**.

Measles, Mischief, and Mishaps
(Book 2)
By L.M. Montgomery,
Adapted by Barbara Davoll

As Sara Stanley continues to spin her wonderful stories, the King cousins get into a load of trouble. First, they convince their neighbor, Sara Ray, to disobey her mother and go to a magic lantern show with them. Then Sara Ray gets very sick with measles and the Story Girl thinks it is all her fault. Then Dan loses a baby he is watching. And if that's not enough, he defiantly eats poison berries and becomes very ill.

SOFTCOVER 0-310-70599-1

Available now at your local bookstore!

Zonder**kidz**.